A BED-STUY STORY

(Pronounced Bed-Sty)

Triumph over Adversity

MAURICE HAMILTON

HAYMAKER PUBLISHING
CHARLOTTE, NORTH CAROLINA

A BED-STUY STORY
(Pronounced Bed-Sty)
Triumph over Adversity

© Copyright March, 2012
Maurice Hamilton

Library of Congress Number: 2011943839
International Standard Book Number: 978-0615501192

Acknowledgments and Dedication

My heartfelt thanks go out to the cadre of persons who have given me their love, support, counsel, challenges, and even doubts. Each and every one of you has enlightened me in some way. I must extend a special thanks and acknowledgment to the editors at CreateSpace.

This book is dedicated to my wife, to my children, and to all those who live in Bed-Stuy and are still struggling to improve that area.

CONTENTS

PREFACE

This book is a novel inspired by my own recollections, experiences, and perspectives from my short stay in Bedford-Stuyvesant, also known as Bed-Stuy, a neighborhood in the New York City borough of Brooklyn. It is not intended to be a definitive history of those events. To protect the privacy of the individuals portrayed in this novel, I have changed names and other identifying characteristics. Some of the individuals portrayed may be composites of more than one person.

INTRODUCTION

While living in "Bed-Stuy", Brooklyn during the 70s, it became abundantly clear to me that winning the struggles to not merely survive, but to prosper, depend on who you think you are, not where you came from or where you live or your age. Cultural conformity aside, who you are and what you can become is defined by the fire within and what ignites it.

This is the story of the fire within a middle-class family living in a nice neighborhood surrounded by chaos and poverty. There is a saying, "When much is given, much is expected." The Wilsons could have stayed in their safe environment and turned a blind eye to their neighbors. Instead, they were profoundly committed to fostering family values, a sense of community, political progress and the pursuit of racial equality. They were determined to use whatever resources available to create jobs, affordable housing and a better quality of life for those struggling in the poor surrounding neighborhoods.

These communities were sometimes very hostile and violent. That did not deter the Wilson's from their goals; it made them more determined. Despite the family's personal tragedy, as a result of their perseverance, and enduring love for humanity, a community was uplifted. This story illustrates the capacity of human beings to triumph over adversity and at the same time help those less fortunate determine their own fates.

"No man was ever endowed with a right without being at the same time saddled with a responsibility."

—Gerald W. Johnson

CHAPTER 1:
GEORGE MAKES HIS ENTRANCE

Friday, April 10, 1970, was an exciting day for the Wilsons. Leonard Jr. arrived home in time for dinner. This was not always the case, especially on Fridays. But today he felt that being home for his family now trumped everything else—his beautiful wife, Harriet, was expecting their third child.

After dinner, as they were doing dishes, he took a long look at his wife of five years. He saw the same strength and beauty in her that he had seen on the day they met. Although having children was not a new thing for them—with Rasheed now four years old and Rachael two—Harriet's belly seemed so much bigger this time around.

Suddenly, Harriet bent over and loudly screamed. "My water just broke!" She yelled, "I need to go now!"

Leonard hurried to get his wife and children into their blue 1970 Buick LeSabre, then off they rushed to St. John's Episcopal Hospital. Although it was only a few blocks away, it seemed like a few miles.

"It's coming, it's coming!" Harriet panted as they entered the emergency entrance. Leonard ran inside, yelling, "Help,

help! My wife is having a baby!" Hospital staff rushed over with a stretcher. They could see they didn't have a second to waste, so they secured Harriet's body to the stretcher and prepared to deliver the baby right there. They told her to relax; to breathe deep, short breaths; and to push the baby forward at the same time. After only about two minutes, the baby popped out on the gurney, letting out a loud cry.

Because they already had a boy and a girl, Leonard and Harriet were not concerned about the child's gender. It was a healthy boy. They decided to give him a strong male name in hopes it would have a positive influence on his life's journey. They considered various names of family members before deciding to name him George, after Harriet's grandfather, George Turner Sr., a highly decorated Korean War hero and retired postal inspector general. After returning home from the service, George Sr. had gotten a job working for the post office, where he'd met and later married Louise Thompson. While working full time, he'd put himself through law school. However, even though he'd passed the bar exam the first time he took it, very few law firms hired blacks at that time. So he'd remained with the post office until his retirement thirty years later, working his way up from a mail room clerk to inspector general. Leonard and Harriet agreed that the name George seemed to fit the eight-pound, five-ounce boy just fine.

The younger George would always be the baby of the family. Leonard and Harriet decided that, along with their other two children, they now had all they could handle, considering their full schedules. Leonard was a high school assistant principal, and Harriet was a math teacher. These positions demanded a lot of their time, including many hours after the workday was over. Plus, they both loved attending their children's PTA meetings, piano recitals, and karate practices and contests. So Harriet had her tubes tied before she left the hospital.

"There is no doubt that it is around the family and the home that all the greatest virtues, the most dominating virtues of human society, are created, strengthen and maintained"

—*Winston Churchill*

CHAPTER 2:
FROM HARLEM TO STUYVESANT HEIGHTS

The Wilsons lived comfortably in their four-story brownstone row house with wrought-iron railings leading up the very steep front steps. Inside, ceramic tiles gave way to oak parquet flooring, with area rugs serving as decoration and floor protectors. Beautiful chandeliers hung from the nine-foot cathedral ceilings, welcoming visitors inside for more lovely surprises. Artwork hung tastefully on the eggshell-colored walls throughout the house. These paintings included Harriet's own work as well as prints by well-known artists, such as Horace Pippin, Jacob Lawrence, Henry Tanner, Vincent Van Gogh, Claude Monet, and Jackson Pollock.

The early-twentieth-century architecture was typical of the homes in this area of Brooklyn. It was truly a middle-class neighborhood. To Leonard, it didn't seem as though five years had passed since they moved here from their third-floor walk-up apartment in Harlem. Although they'd loved the many familiar and cultural attributes of Harlem—such as the convenient distance to college buddies, the Arturo

Schomburg library, and the social electricity of 125th Street—
they'd wanted to get away from the crowds, the noise, and the
trash-littered streets, not to mention the daily crime they'd
often witnessed. They'd wanted a better environment for
themselves and their children. Brooklyn felt more like home
than Harlem ever had.

The Wilsons' surroundings were a big contrast to their
old Harlem neighborhood. They settled in a section of
Brooklyn called Bedford-Stuyvesant (Bed-Stuy). Commonly
pronounced Bed-Sty, it was actually an area made up of
four neighborhoods: Bedford, Stuyvesant Heights, Ocean
Hill (Brownsville), and Weeksville. Bedford and Stuyvesant
Heights became one neighborhood, thus generating the new
name Bedford- Stuyvesant, or Bed-Stuy.

In the Styvesant-Heights section, the crime rate was
very low, and the streets were quiet and clean. Another
attraction was the different shade trees—poplar, red maple,
magnolia, and flowering Kwanzan cherry—that lined each
block. These trees were especially beautiful when in full
bloom. Many successful blacks had moved into this area
from Harlem because the crime rate was so low. It was a well-
structured, middle-class neighborhood, and the community
was beginning to establish a strong political, educational,
and economic base. The neighbors were friendly and helpful
toward each other.

The Wilsons' home was in Stuyvesant Heights; their
parents lived close by in Weeksville, where Leonard and
Harriet had spent their childhoods. The Wilsons' place of
worship, First Baptist Church, was located there as well.
Leonard and Harriet were both Baptist; the religion been
passed on to them by their parents, who'd explained
how the Baptist church was intertwined with the history of

the African American struggle toward freedom in the United States. Their parents had also taught them that the rhythm and blues root of some of today's music began in the black church. The church was a place where civil rights leaders met and planned strategies to gain their freedom from Jim Crow laws in the South and in the North. Though Leonard and Harriet had grown up attending the same church, they hadn't started dating until their senior year in high school.

They'd moved to Harlem to be close to Washington University, where they both received graduate degrees. Harriet had earned her first master's degree in education and a second in administration and supervision. Leonard had earned his PhD in education. Their decision to move back to Brooklyn had also been influenced by the interesting history their parents had told them about the area. Weeksville had been named after James Weeks, a free African American entrepreneur who'd bought land in 1838 and sold it to other black settlers, who began immigrating from the South and settling in Weeksville and nearby Carsville in the 1830s and '40s. [1]

Over the years the demographics of the neighborhood had changed dramatically. During the 1860s and '70s, wealthy Dutch and German descendants moved into the area. It changed again from 1880 to about 1920 because of the construction of elevated subway lines, which gave easy access to downtown Brooklyn and Manhattan. [2]

At that time, the area attracted Jews, Italians, West Indians, Irish, and many other ethnic groups. Whites eventually moved out and left the area to black Southerners and immigrants from various parts of the Caribbean. [3]

While sharing a little history of Bed Stuy with Leonard and Harriet, Grandpa George also told them that during the 1950s and '60s, black people could not buy homes anywhere they wanted in Brooklyn because there were far too many whites who felt that blacks were an inferior group of people and did not want to allow them access to the American dream. Being aware of this, blacks invested their time, money, and energy into revitalizing their own neighborhoods and making them an example of what blacks could achieve. They made some progress.

According to Grandpa George, it has been that way for years. A key factor in high unemployment is that many white people in power would rather hire a foreigner than an American black. Grandpa once told Harriet that right after World War II many black soldiers returned home to find that the very people for whom they fought were replacing them on the job front with foreigners and they were able to assimilate as American citizens with all the benefits. African Americans were forced to live as second class citizens, which meant there was major restrictions on where they lived and access to the American dream. Another reason for this high crime rate was the introduction of heroin and cocaine by white drug dealers into the already depressed neighborhood.

At that time, black men could not vote in political elections in the North or especially in the South, because most of them were still slaves. After passage of the Fifteenth Amendment in 1870, which gave black men the right to vote, Ku Klux Klansmen and Jim Crow laws often kept them from the voting polls. Blacks did not get much support from the law when they tried to vote until the civil rights movement during the 1960s.

The Wilsons were proud to learn that in 1965, Andrew W. Cooper, a journalist from Bedford-Stuyvesant, protested against racial gerrymandering by filing a lawsuit under the Voting Rights Act.

Cooper prevailed. His win resulted in the creation of New York's Twelfth Congressional District, which in 1968 elected Shirley Chisholm, the first black woman in the U.S. Congress. [4]

Previously white lawmakers had divided up the Bed-Stuy area for the special advantage of having the majority of votes over blacks. They wanted to make sure blacks never controlled their own districts and force blacks to rely on begging and pleading with the white congressmen to fund vital neighborhood projects. The lawsuit asserted that Bedford-Stuyvesant was divided among five congressional districts, each represented by a white Congress member. [5]

Also during the 1960s, the Wilsons got a chance to see Senator Robert F. Kennedy as he toured Bed-Stuy's dilapidated streets. His presence and support became the catalyst for the Bedford-Stuyvesant Restoration Corporation. Known as the Restoration, it was launched by Kennedy and other national leaders as a model for community development. Initially funded by foundations, it is still in operation. [6]

The Wilsons as well as other concerned residents in Stuyvesant Heights were hopeful that the Restoration Corporation would lift the worst areas of the community out of poverty. Although lots of money and expertise were channeled into the neighborhood through this organization, and it had some impact on the community as a whole, it failed to successfully rehabilitate the worst area of Bedford-Stuyvesant. [7]

While addressing a community meeting, Leonard outlined the steps that would be required to successfully rehabilitate the area: Action is needed on many fronts: first, there has to be affordable housing, job training programs, training on how to become entrepreneurs, parenting classes, child and youth mentoring programs. As soon as possible the community needs to be able to represent themselves and address their problems. They need to do like other successful neighborhoods and learn to negotiate with their own local government and utilities for the infrastructure and services to which they are entitled."

The Stuyvesant Heights neighborhood within Bed-Stuy, on the other hand, was moving forward and establishing many vital resources. It included public community centers for youth and senior citizens, beautiful Gothic-style churches, drug stores, doctors' and dentists' offices, and a functional school board. Strong community support resulted in successful neighborhood schools. The high school graduation rate for students living in this area was the same as it was in white middle-class schools. The Restoration played a major role in making this happen.

According to Leonard, under the leadership of Franklin A. Thomas, president and CEO of Bedford-Stuyvesant Restoration Corporation (1967-1977), the Restoration raised $63 million in public and private funds—including a significant amount from the Ford Foundation. The Restoration built three apartment complexes and erected a 200,000 square foot shopping center. It rehabilitated 400 brownstone units, established the Billie Holiday Theater, helped to start or expand 120 businesses in the area, and developed a $21 million mortgage pool. Under Thomas's leadership, the Restoration Corporation lured an IBM facility into the neighborhood, placed 7,000 residents in jobs and helped engender a positive feeling among the neighborhood's residents. Perhaps most importantly, Thomas's Restoration Corporation became a model for the hundreds of community-based redevelopment corporations that would later come into being around the country.

In addition, the neighborhood was filled with black professional role models: lawyers, doctors, teachers, school administrators, social workers, real-estate agents, and other professionals and businesspeople. They all went to the neighborhood churches and socialized with each other at the local bowling alleys, billiard halls, social clubs, taverns, and restaurants. They had mutual investments in each other and in the community as a whole. Many retired teachers volunteered at libraries and tutored students in a variety of elementary to secondary school subjects. Churches also offered free tutoring after school. Education was revered.

Given its history and current progress, the atmosphere in Stuyvesant Heights was a dream comes true for the Wilsons. From all appearances, they established a lifestyle on the same economic level as that of many white people in Brooklyn.

"First it is necessary to stand on your own two feet. But the minute a man finds himself in that position, the next thing he should do is reach out his arms"

—*Kristin Hunter*

CHAPTER 3:
A BED-STUY STORY

A few blocks southeast in the community lies another side to the beautifully structured and manicured paradise. Some areas adjacent to Stuyvesant Heights were just as bad as or even worse than the neighborhood the Wilsons had left behind. These sections were filled with abandoned buildings, filthy streets, high crime rates, drug deals, and felons. These residents had stopped dreaming of the good life. The poor section of Bedford-Stuyvesant was once known as that nation's largest low-income community. [8]

George had traveled through this area with his parents, but had no personal knowledge of hard living.

Those who lived in this section of Bed-Stuy experienced a much harsher reality. Mary H. Manoni begins her 1973 book, *Bedford-Stuyvesant: The Anatomy of a Central City Community*, by asking the question: "Why would anyone want to live there? [9]

One possible answer might be that people want to be part of a community where they are at least considered an equal in the human chain and as such deserve the same rights and privileges as everyone else. They deserve this in spite of the fact they are black, poor, and ignored by those who are in a position to help them or who won't because of their own issues."

People who did not know anyone in Bed-Stuy and did not absolutely have to go there were wise to stay out. The police encouraged outsiders to stay out of these neighborhoods, because if something of a criminal nature happened, no one would come forward as a witness out of fear for their own lives. The unwritten "no-snitch" rule was imposed by gang leaders, drug dealers, and other criminals in the neighborhood. Many crimes went unsolved, leaving murderers, rapists, and drug dealers to rule the streets. At a community meeting, some residents argued that the main reason for so much crime was the high unemployment rate, contending that it forced residents into a life of crime.

"If there is anything that we wish to change in the child, we should first examine it and see whether it is not something that could better be changed in ourselves."

—C. G. Jung

CHAPTER 4:
RAP BECOMES THE NEW YOUTH CULTURE

Residents in this poor area of Bed-Stuy became creative and made tough choices to survive. Those who were unemployed or underemployed devised ways of hustling to make ends meet. Some received food stamps and welfare, but, as this was not enough to survive on, they found other ways to get money. They would dry cars for tips at a carwash; scour for scrap metal to sell; gamble, usually with dice; play cards; shoot pool; and play illegal lottery numbers. Some sold drugs and alcoholic beverages from their cars or homes, and others drove the gypsy cabs that cruised areas not served by yellow cabs. Some set up informal neighborhood child care centers or sold stolen jewelry or designer clothes.

Those who could afford it found another way to feel good about themselves: with their hustle money, some people, especially the youths, would buy designer clothes or expensive sneakers by K-Swiss, Reebok, Nike, and Adidas. They would also spend their money on expensive jewelry. These riches made them the "famous" idols of their neighborhood.

Clothes muggings began to occur in which young men

and women were robbed of designer shoes and clothes. They were told, typically at gunpoint, to "take it off and give it to me!"

During the 1980s, it was also cool to show off one's hairstyle, even during the cold New York winters. Popular hairstyles for men ranged from the very short, such as the haircuts worn by Eddie Murphy and David "Sinbad" Adkins, to the long Jheri curl worn by the King of Pop, Michael Jackson. The rap duo Kid 'N Play popularized the high-top fade. Don King wore a unique afro—it looked as though he were being electrocuted and the current were running through his hair!

Realizing rap's influence on kids' fashion—and attitudes— Leonard and Harriet had to confront the issue of whether to allow their children to follow the hip-hop movement.

When George was fourteen years old, he came home one day and said, "Mom, I need a pair of Adidas sneakers and a New York Yankees cap." She replied, "George, I know you're now a teenager, and you want the freedom to make choices in what you wear, but as we allow you more freedom, you will have to assume more responsibilities. That includes making reasonable and responsible requests from us. We cannot just buy everything you want or buy you something because other kids are wearing it. I'll discuss this matter with your father; as your parents, we'll decide if this is in your best interest."

George's parents allowed his older brother to wear a shorter version of the Kid 'N Play hairstyle, and his sister's fashion sense was just a little on the provocative side. The Wilsons were trying to walk a thin line with their children's style of dress. They knew if they demanded an absolutely conservative style, their children would strongly reject it. So the Wilsons carefully chose areas in which they could allow their children some room to fit in without getting teased, hurt, or even killed for the clothes they wore. It was not an easy task. Meanwhile, George and Rachael would sometimes shed tears to get their parents to see things their way.

In a conversation with his dad, George said, "Kids have to look tough or they'll get beat up and taken advantage of."

His father's response was, "Son, you will never please everybody. In most cases, it's not worth trying. Just remember you cannot be everything to all the people all the time."

Leonard and Harriet had these types of conversations with their children often, but it always took a while for each child to process the information. Their children listened and usually embraced their parents' values after carefully weighing the pros and cons.

Instead of buying the clothing items George had requested, the Wilsons talked him into letting them buy an Atari 2600 with joysticks. This way, he could play the video game at home with a family member or invite friends over to play. Although the Wilsons could have easily afforded to buy the things George wanted, they also knew they had to draw the line somewhere. Wearing those clothes could cause problems for him and everyone else. So they decided to reward him for being a good child and great student by buying him something to enjoy at home, where they would not have to worry that someone was going to rob or to hurt him. With that reward, though, they also gave George a new responsibility in the household: collecting all the trash and making sure it was put out on trash days. This had been Rachael's job, but she was made responsible for keeping the windows clean. Rasheed was in charge of cleaning the bathroom.

"It's not only children who grow. Parents do too. As much as we watch to see what our children do with their lives, they are watching us to see what we do with ours. I can't tell my children to reach for the sun. All I can do is reach for it, myself."

—Joyce Maynard

CHAPTER 5:
SOME YOUNG HUSTLERS MADE IT BIG

Young people figured out a way to hustle as well. Disco music was replaced by rap music in neighborhoods with young black people. Crowds at rap contests became larger and larger. The rappers made money, and some became stars and role models. Rap music blasted from boom boxes everywhere in Bed-Stuy.

Rap was also used as a weapon. Rappers would sing about shooting government officials, crooked police officers, and other public figures. They would also "dis" each other through a rap, a shortened form of "disparage" or "disrespect"; either way, the expression meant to put someone in his or her place.

George was an attention seeker. He was good at writing rap music rhymes, so he gained a considerable following when he joined rap contests. George thought he had realized his dreams. He came home from school one day and declared, "Mom, I'm going to be a famous rapper."

The Wilsons grew very concerned about George, who began wearing gold chains and earning money with his newly discovered skills, "spitting rhymes" as a rapper. His activities began to have a negative effect on his grades in school. The tangible benefits he received from rapping were making it difficult for his parents to convince him that this may not be the best career choice for him, and that, in reality, he was losing ground in the effort to become a success for the rest of his life.

George began thinking about his parents' concerns when he was robbed. Although he was a third-degree black belt in karate, he was outnumbered and unprepared for the thugs who put a gun to his head and took all his money and jewelry. He told his brother about the incident and said, "I'm going to get a gun to protect myself."

Rasheed reminded his little brother, "Your best weapon is between your ears, and that's your brain. If you have to go through all that, maybe it's not worth it. You are being robbed because of the gold chains and the other flashy things you wear. You don't need a gun. You need to change the way you dress and stop trying to be a thug. That's not your life. You don't have to hustle the way those people do, so stop trying to be someone you're not. If you keep on, you're going to get killed over some bullshit. Mom, Dad, Ray, and I all love you, so get yourself back on track before it's too late."

George usually listened to his older brother's advice, or at least seriously considered it, but he wasn't sure he wanted to give up his newfound fame just yet.

Another thriving hustle involved peddling bootlegged mix tapes and knock-offs of name-brand clothes. Being a DJ at a party was also a good way to hustle for money and possibly a way to become famous. Those were some of the "soft" and safest hustles.

A huge group of homeless people lived in Bed-Stuy. Some were veterans. Many of these people collected plastic soda and beer bottles daily and took them to be recycled and redeemed for cash. Others stood at busy intersections and washed the windshields of cars sitting at stoplights, hoping to get a few coins or even a buck or two. Sometimes these hustlers got paid a little change, but sometimes they didn't get a dime. Drivers complained, and eventually it became illegal to solicit money this way.

Other illegal hustles included pimping, prostitution, gambling, and playing illegal numbers. Numbers is a form of gambling in which a bettor attempts to pick three or four digits to match those that will be randomly drawn twice that day, once in the afternoon and once in the evening. The gambler places the bet with a bookie at a bar, corner store, pool hall, or other privately owned joint that acts as a betting parlor. Residents could also place bets with a numbers runner in the neighborhood without ever having to leave their stoops. These people called in the collected betting slips to the headquarters, also known as a numbers bank or policy bank. If someone had chosen the numbers that were drawn, he or she would win, much like the modern (and legal) lottery system.

Poverty, prostitution, gambling, and drugs (especially crack cocaine) were a perfect mix to create high crime rates and violence in any neighborhood. Many young people eventually learned that this lifestyle was definitely not preparing them for the mainstream workforce. As a result, upwardly mobile families moved out of Bed-Stuy as soon as they could, leaving behind empty houses and a neighborhood that, under those circumstances, remained a haven for poverty.

Many residents of Stuyvesant Heights refused to give up and made tireless efforts to change the culture of these surrounding areas. They knew it would be in their best interest to do so; if not, the situation could have easily spread, like cancer, into their neighborhoods. This burden was placed on the shoulders of everyone who was able to help, especially the clergy, educators, politicians, parents, and the police.

One issue was that area did not support enough industry to employ residents. The Brooklyn Navy Yard hired a lot of people from these disadvantaged neighborhoods, but there was not enough work to go around. With the high level of dropouts, undereducated, and beaten-down people, the area needed the kinds of businesses that would offer jobs for low- to medium-skilled workers.

Adding to this problem was the fact that more and more immigrants were moving into the neighborhood and competing for the same jobs. Some immigrants worked with leaders to help alleviate the problem. Others resented being forced to live among poor blacks, believing that they were better than these uneducated Americans. Some married African Americans to gain citizenship and later divorced them to bring their spouses to the United States from their home countries. Other immigrants came to the United States with marketable skills in business or industry and strong work ethics.

Leonard, like many other responsible and dedicated community leaders, felt that the area had potential; he and others like him would do what was necessary to realize that potential. Whenever he was called to help, Leonard never hesitated to offer his services. He would help with writing grants, creating budgets, and bringing into the poor neighborhood other influential people who were willing to help strengthen the community.

Unfortunately, when he and other well-dressed professional black people came into the community, their polished and refined looks made them prime targets for robbery. Thugs looking for easy prey would spot them right away. Drug dealers and others who made criminal activity a way of life viewed Dr. Wilson and others who tried to help as outsiders who did not belong there.

"Never doubt that a small group of thoughtful, committed citizens can change the world. Indeed, it is the only thing that ever has."

—*Margaret Mead*

CHAPTER 6:
DR. WILSON BELIEVED LEADERSHIP MEANT SERVICE TO THE COMMUNITY

Leonard received his graduate degrees while working his way through the New York City Board of Education. He gained a reputation for innovative, creative thinking to solve the problems unique to urban settings. Years spent teaching young urban students showed Leonard that they definitely needed options. He believed that one set of educational standards—courses geared toward the college-bound—did not work for all high school students. Some students might not want to go to college immediately after graduating; some might choose the military, others might go directly into the workforce full time, and some might choose to become entrepreneurs.

The school system needed to offer not only an academic diploma for those who wanted to go to college and a technology education diploma for those who wanted to enter the trades (such as automotive or mechanical) but also a general diploma for those who were unsure of their long-term goals.

Leonard believed that leadership meant service to the community; he was a true hands-on, people person. His greatest asset was being able to communicate his ideas. His visions were presented with clarity, so he could easily persuade an audience to support his viewpoints and philosophies. By the time he was thirty-six, he had worked fourteen years in the New York City school system—ten years as a high school math teacher and four years as an assistant principal. He was among the top educators in the city and became established as a strong and effective leader. He became known for getting things done on time and bringing clarity and closure to issues. His participatory style of leadership helped him draw support from parents, his staff, and colleagues. He made decisions by getting all the necessary information and input from the parties involved, drawing a conclusion, and putting things into action. He always had a plan. A slogan he often used was, "People who fail to plan are, in actuality, planning to fail."

Harriet, two years younger than her husband, was a principal at an elementary school in their neighborhood. Like Leonard, she was always organized and well-dressed. They both wore their neatly cut afros with pride. Both of their parents were Southerners who placed a high value on education. Washington University was an integral part of the Wilsons' lives, because this is where they'd become inseparable partners for life.

They'd married on June 6, 1960. They were friends and nourished their relationship by spending quality time together no matter how busy and complicated their lives became. This might mean a movie, a concert, or just strolling through the streets in the East Village on a Saturday night, browsing stores. They were determined to fulfill each other's needs and keep their romance alive. They loved each other very much.

After George was born, Harriet took a leave of absence from the NYC Board of Education—her intentions were to be on leave for one year. The Wilsons were concerned because Leonard's work schedule was getting busier and they didn't want to neglect their children for advancement in their careers or for money. So Harriet temporarily became a stay-at-home mom.

By that time, Leonard earned enough money to maintain their lifestyle. Harriet was able to do more of what she really enjoyed, such as preparing wholesome, healthy meals for the family; giving more attention to her baby, George; and spending more time individually with Rasheed and Rachael. She also enjoyed helping them with homework and other school projects as well as attending PTA meetings, karate classes and matches, and music lessons and piano recitals for little Rasheed.

In the past, Harriet's and Leonard's parents had helped by watching the children when they could. During the week, though, while the Wilsons had lived in Harlem, Harriet had hired a twenty-three-year-old college student named Darlene to help them. She attended New York University during the day and needed all the extra money she could get, because attending college and paying rent in New York was expensive. She turned out to be an excellent babysitter.

"It is better to be prepared for an opportunity and not have one than to have one and not be prepared."

—*Whitney M. Young*

CHAPTER 7:
DR. WILSON BECOMES DEPUTY CHANCELLOR

A strange turn of events brought an unexpected surprise to the Wilsons, one that moved them even closer to the American dream.

The New York City school system's deputy chancellor, Patrick Fahey, a married man with three children, became caught up in an adulterous affair with a married colleague and could no longer function in his position. His beautiful wife, Tammy, vowed in a TV interview that she would stick by her husband and together they would seek marital counseling. However, three months later, the situation worsened when the other woman Fahey was involved with claimed she was pregnant with his child.

Fahey could not avoid hearing the story on radio or seeing it unfold on every television station. Tammy was a strong woman and truly wanted to be in his corner, but she could not overcome her hurt, frustration, and anger. She didn't want to push her husband too far, but she had to ask him, "Why did you do this to us?"

His response was, "I don't know." He knew she needed

a better reason than that, but he could not think of one that would ease her pain or put things back the way they were. Fahey became so distraught that he went into his bedroom, put a loaded .38-caliber pistol under his chin, and pulled the trigger. He died instantly.

Although grief-stricken, the school system's chancellor, Albert "Al" Weinstein, began to search for Fahey's replacement. Leonard was one of six candidates interviewed by a panel that included members of the school board, parents, and other city officials. Leonard stood head and shoulders above the other candidates. Al had worked with Leonard on many occasions and had always liked him. As a trial run, he requested that Leonard speak at many of his school board meetings and at other leadership conferences.

Leonard won the appointment and became New York City's first African American deputy chancellor. For many blacks in the city, especially those living in Stuyvesant Heights, this achievement was a huge step in the right direction for the community. Many of those living in the poorer section were proud and believed that Leonard's appointment gave them hope for their neighborhood. For far too long, the city had ignored the special needs of a community suffering from alienation and neglect.

Leonard remembered his own meager beginnings when someone once asked him, "Why are you so passionate about the people of Bed-Stuy?" He simply said, "But for the grace of God, there go I." He remembered the days when he and Harriet barely had enough money to pay their bills, to attend college, and to buy food to eat. He often reminisced about the times they'd had to hustle to make things work, like others who were poor and felt left behind by mainstream America. The couple would practice dancing together and go to a nightclub that hosted dance contests—and they often won.

They'd also give weekly philosophical- discussion parties to pay the rent. A five-dollar entry fee per partygoer yielded hors d'œuvres, wine, sparkling grape juice, apple cider, and a chance to see and to purchase Harriet's large framed photographs and paintings. In addition to raising rent money, the party's purpose was to explore important topics, such as:

What is the difference between force and persuasion?

Do you have a mind?

How do you know, at this very moment, that you are not in a dream state and are truly in a state of reality?

What is the difference between love and romance?

What is the difference between assertiveness and aggression?

What is the difference between pain and suffering?

Are you sure everything that you believe is true?

If not, why do you still believe?

Can you prove your beliefs are true?

Their little one-bedroom apartment would quickly become crowded with as many as fifteen college students, and the meetings would sometimes last until 3:00 a.m.

The most important aspect of the parties was that the Wilsons had a great time socializing with friends and were intellectually stimulated, but they also earned enough money to pay the rent each month.

So Leonard and Harriet had a lot of empathy for those living in the poor section of Bed-Stuy. Although Leonard was an important figure in the community, he was a humble person who believed it was his duty to do whatever he could to help others make the transition from a bad situation to a good one.

"Leaders establish the vision for the future and set the strategy for getting it there; they cause change. They motivate and inspire others to go in the right direction and they, along with everyone else, sacrifice to get there."

—*John Kotter*

CHAPTER 8:
A GREAT LOSS

One hot Saturday afternoon in July 1985, Leonard and a community group had just finished a very important meeting held in a neighborhood public school. He ran into Reverend Mitchell "Mitch" Greene, a well-known minister and senior pastor of Beacon Chapel Baptist Church, located in the poorest section of the community. Mitch was proud of the progress made by his church, so he invited Leonard to visit Beacon Chapel and its relatively new facility, the Bed-Stuy Youth Center. Although the center had been in operation for two years, lots of improvements were underway. It had taken kids off the streets and created a basketball team and tennis and chess clubs. The center also offered a tutoring service for students in secondary school.

Although they attended different churches, Mitch and Leonard were childhood friends. Mitch asked Leonard to make suggestions for additional improvements at the youth center. Although the facility was located in the worst part of Bed-Stuy, Leonard didn't hesitate for a moment and agreed to meet Mitch there.

Mitch loved to show off the new after-school community center; he believed it was a place of hope for kids from ages twelve to twenty-one. Here, kids could get help with schoolwork. Some children came just to eat and play ping-pong, to shoot pool, to jump rope, or to participate in other team and individual sports. However, the youth were also required to take advantage of the free tutoring and to show improvement in their grades. The center had a large study hall where retired teachers were on hand to help students in all subject areas.

That warm summer night, however, would turn into a nightmare. Everyone had left the center except Mitch and Leonard. As they were getting ready to leave, two young men knocked on the door and rushed in, brandishing guns and demanding money. Mitch and Leonard gave the gunmen what they had in their pockets, but the thieves demanded more. They forced Mitch to open the office safe, which held only about $200 in cash and some personal checks. One of the gunmen became impatient and shot Leonard in the head; the other man shot Mitch in the stomach and chest. The thugs then ran out into the street, jumped into a waiting car, and sped away, leaving the center's front door wide open.

Two neighbors, Butch and Skip, had been sitting on the stoop across the street, drinking beer, smoking cigarettes, and talking about who they thought might win the next day's game between the Yankees and the Mets. The men heard what they thought were shots fired and saw the two thugs running and then driving away.

Butch and Skip ran inside the center and heard Mitch's groans. They used the office phone to call 911, but the police and paramedics arrived too late. Leonard had died instantly. Mitch lasted a few minutes longer, dying en route to the hospital. The witnesses were able to give a clear description of the two gunmen, because the criminals had not covered their faces. Butch and Skip were also able to describe the getaway car, a red 1985 Mustang, although they were not able to describe the driver. When the police learned that one of these dead men was a city official, officers came from everywhere, leaving no stone unturned to find the criminals. It took fewer than thirty minutes to catch the suspects.

Police usually gave crime in the area a low priority. However, this crime—which included the murder of a city official—was going to be widely publicized in every newspaper in the city. The visibility of this crime led police to work quickly.

When the police arrested two of the suspects, they were sure they had the right guys, because Butch and Skip had described them in detail. One was a muscular, six-foot-tall, dark-skinned black man in his mid-to late twenties. The other man was a few inches taller, with a slender build and much lighter skin. The big, muscular man was wearing a blue and white Yankee baseball cap turned backward, a blue and white plaid shirt with the tails hanging outside his blue jeans, and Adidas sneakers. He was later identified as twenty-eight-year-old Qualeb Poppytail, a career criminal who had committed several felonies, including attempted murder, assault with a deadly weapon, rape, and robbery. He'd been recently paroled after serving time in prison for a rape charge.

The other assailant was Jonathan "Moneymaker" Woodhead, age twenty-four, who wore a Boston Red Sox cap also turned backward and a light blue shirt with the shirttails hanging outside his khaki pants. Moneymaker had a criminal record, but it was for misdemeanors, such as petty larceny, smoking marijuana in public, and having a small amount of marijuana on him each time he was caught. It was later learned that he thought that if he hung out with Qualeb, he would get a lot of respect from other thugs in the 'hood.

When the police caught the suspects, they put the K-9 dogs on them and roughed them up a bit, just to let them know that a city official was one of their boys. The police also knew they could do whatever they wanted to with the suspects and get away with it. In situations like this senseless murder, the Bed-Stuy community usually supported the police in whatever action they took. The getaway driver was still in the Mustang as the other men were being arrested, handcuffed, and put into the back of the patrol car. The police repeatedly asked the driver to get out of his car with his hands in the air. Suddenly, he opened the door, firing a .38-caliber gun at the police. The officers took cover behind their cruisers and fired back, striking the driver five times in the chest and head. No police officers were hurt.

The suspect was dead before the ambulance arrived. He was later identified as twenty-seven-year-old Peanut Williams. Peanut was no stranger to police; he had a long record dating back sixteen years and had just been released from state prison the same day as Qualeb for aggravated assault. He'd served time for hitting a Korean grocery store owner, Dim Young Kim, in the head with a glass quart bottle of Colt 45 beer. The store owner later died from the injury, but Peanut had claimed self-defense. He'd received a six-month sentence because the judge, Robert Goldberg, did not have a witness or evidence proving Mr. Kim's death was not the result of self-defense. The only witness, a thirteen-year-old African American girl, Tootsie Brown, said she saw the store owner come from behind the counter, swinging a baseball bat at Peanut. Peanut then hit him in the head with the beer bottle and left the store. Fearing for her life, she ran out of the store in the opposite direction from Peanut.

Peanut might have gotten away without serving any time if he hadn't told Judge Goldberg that Kim had probably mistaken him for someone who'd robbed him in the past: "These foreigners come into our neighborhood and rob people every day by jacking up the price of the merchandise 300 percent, selling beer and cigarettes to underage children, and selling tons of candy, sodas, and ice cream. There is very little healthy food in these stores. They get away with robbing and destroying our people because the nearest supermarket is two miles away."

He went on to tell the judge, "Mr. Kim and others like him do not live in our neighborhood; they just extract the money from it and do not put anything back. We live in the projects; they live in nice houses far away from our neighborhood. So they come here to rob us to support their lifestyles and destroy ours."

Judge Goldberg asked Peanut, "Are you saying this man's murder was justified because he did business in your neighborhood?"

"No, Your Honor, I am saying that he is allowed to rob us and nothing is done about it, but when he gets robbed someone has to serve time for it. There's a double standard here," Peanut responded.

That's when the judge gave Peanut a six-month sentence for aggravated assault. Peanut did not know how to defend himself, so he went to jail. He should not have gone to jail for stating what he believed; sentencing should have been based solely on the evidence in his case. He felt this sentence had been a violation of his civil rights, but some in the community felt the sentencing judge had been too lenient—had Peanut spent more time in jail, maybe Leonard would still be alive.

The handiwork of these three criminals triggered a major

step backward in the community. Two major players in the neighborhood's development had been permanently lost, causing irreparable damage to a fragile but promising area. The dire loss of leadership, coupled with unconcealed evil, had damaged the community's growing air of optimism about change.

Many people who were dedicated to strengthening the area now reevaluated their outlook. They began to fear that nothing could be done to alter the course of Bed-Stuy's further decline into poverty and violence. The question they asked was, "Is saving this area worth the price we're paying?" After all, the results were slow to develop and never made the difference that was so desperately needed.

At Dr. Wilson's funeral, Reverend Ray Davis, PhD, Leonard's minister of the last fifteen years, asked the question, "Isn't it ironic that two people Dr. Wilson came over to help were the ones who killed him?" But, Rev. Davis added, "We must continue to complete his great work and win the battle against violent crime, drug dealing, and prostitution in this neighborhood. Through his great legacy, he will secure our future if we stay on track and continue the work he has done."

Rev. Davis further stated that these kinds of actions had to be replaced with better ways to educate the area's children and adults, many of whom had given up on getting jobs: "We have to continue to work together to make their struggling neighborhood as successful as Stuyvesant Heights." Otherwise, he cautioned, "It will be the other way around; this whole area will be lost."

He went on to say, "No government is going to come down here and fix this problem. However, those in political power can and will help if a community can show a significant improvement created by the residents. Many politicians want to be part of a winning team effort so that they can claim credit and get reelected to office."

Getting things back on track would require a Herculean effort, because the neighborhood drug dealers and some white politicians from other areas felt it was a bad idea to invest in revitalization of the area. Drug dealers were more willing to give financial help to many people, so some residents felt indebted to the drug dealers and defended their right to be in the neighborhood. The problem now was, could they get enough people on board and create strategies to challenge and to defeat the monster in this poor neighborhood that threatened the community as a whole?

During the weeks that passed after the funerals, a group of neighborhood leaders from Stuyvesant Heights met at the same community center where Mitch and Leonard had been murdered to discuss plans to move forward with more resources and a will to win. They made it clear to all in attendance that if the community failed to solve the problem, it would eventually spill over into other areas like a plague and could become the worst of any of the five boroughs of New York City.

"Healing takes courage, and we all have courage, even if we have to dig a little to find it."

—*Tori Amos*

CHAPTER 9:
HOW WAS HARRIET DOING A YEAR LATER?

In the year that passed after Leonard's death, Harriet and the children grieved their loss and tried to move on with their lives. During the days and weeks following the death of her husband, Harriet was inconsolable at times. If not for her children, she often said, "I do not know how I could go on." She thought about how different things had been when she'd lost her grandparents five years prior to Leonard's death.

First there was Grandpa George, who'd lived a full life and died at age ninety-six of pancreatic cancer. He'd endured the painful and agonizing illness for six months, which gave him the chance to go through the stages of death as identified by well-known psychiatrist Dr. Elisabeth Kübler-Ross. Her 1969 book, *On Death and Dying*, defines those stages as denial, anger, bargaining, depression, and acceptance. [9]

In the denial stage, Grandpa had said that this was another one of life's trials. After all, he had experienced many rough episodes in his lifetime and lived through them all. "Why should this time be any different?" he'd thought.

Then the anger stage came. After a couple of months,

family members and Grandpa George's doctors had helped him see that this was a serious and terminal illness. He'd become angry, because he felt the timing was wrong. His concern had been about who would protect Louise, his wife of sixty-three years. He'd promised her that he would be there for her until she died, so he'd been very hurt at the prospect of breaking that promise and leaving her without him.

Next, he'd thought that he could strike a deal with God by promising to give up some of his bad habits, like swearing, and giving more service to the church—all if God would only give him a little more time. He had felt conflicted regarding whom he should believe: his doctors, who were telling him that their prognosis of death was a reality, or his belief that God would give him more time if he mended his ways. He'd begun experiencing more pain than ever before, so he'd become depressed but had eventually begun to accept the inevitable. He'd realized he was nearing his end on Earth, and nothing was going to change that.

He'd died in August 1980. Just three months later, Louise had become ill and died from a severe case of pneumonia. She'd gone through similar stages before her death. Both of these family members had been elderly, so their deaths were expected. In Leonard's case, his death had been completely sudden, catching everyone by surprise. This aspect made it more difficult to process, because it was harder to accept the thought that he was gone forever. He'd been a young, mentally and physically healthy man with so much energy. Harriet had expected to grow old with him and enjoy parenting their wonderful children together.

Harriet knew that raising children as a single parent would be difficult, but she felt blessed by the almighty God to have generally nice children who happened to be brilliant. Rasheed was in his second year at Washington University on a full presidential scholarship. The scholarship program had been established in 1964 by executive order of the president to recognize and to honor some of the nation's most distinguished graduating high school seniors. Rasheed had decided to follow in his parents' footsteps by taking university-level math and political-science courses at the college. So it had been no surprise to his parents and everyone else that he would have a double major. He had a strong urge to pursue a career in corporate law.

The tall, handsome, athletic-looking, well-spoken, and articulate young man reminded everyone that his father was still alive through him. He had the look of a classic college student, sporting plaid sweaters, khakis, Hush Puppies, and a neatly trimmed afro. Rasheed's polished looks could be deceiving though; he was a tenth-degree black belt in karate, as were many of his friends. He was the firstborn and readily accepted responsibility for upholding the family's values and traditions, which made him serious when it came to defending his siblings.

Rasheed was not without some character flaws. He had been born June 25, 1966. When his father had been alive, he'd thought he could get his parents to ease their rules a little. He'd graduated from high school a few days before his seventeenth birthday and then had waited for a time when he was alone with his parents to ask, "Will it be okay if we have beer at my party tomorrow night? We promise we won't get drunk or anything like that."

Leonard and Harriet had looked at each other for a moment and simultaneously said, "No."

Rasheed stood his ground. "Why not? I promise we won't cause any trouble."

His parents' response: "Because we said so!"

On several occasions Harriet had come home and caught Rasheed sneaking his girlfriend, Ebony, out the back door. She'd warned him about it a couple of times and finally told his dad, who threatened to throw Rasheed out of the house if the behavior didn't stop.

If Rasheed didn't like a particular karate competitor, he would hold the wooden board the person was about to strike with his hand so the person would hit it across the grain, making the wood almost impossible to break and causing his competitor's hand to be injured or broken. Rasheed was a typical teenager, with his good and bad qualities.

Rasheed was never a gang member, but he did have a group of childhood friends who were often referred to as "the Brainy Crew." They all had an IQ above one hundred sixty, and the seven girls and five boys, including Ebony and Rasheed, all naturally gravitated toward each other. They would get teased by classmates for getting high grades on exams without much effort, but they knew they could always count on each other for support. They understood each other and knew each other's faults, strengths, and idiosyncrasies.

Rachael had graduated with honors from Bentley High School in Manhattan. Some of the brightest students from all over the city attended the prestigious school. The school's goal was to prepare students for responsible citizenship and leadership roles in the global community. Rachael was valedictorian of her class. Like her mother, she was blessed with intelligence and good looks. The only concern her mother had while Rachael was in high school was that she sometimes attracted unwarranted attention by dressing a little too suggestively. Even Rachael would become annoyed with some boys who "overreacted" to her style of clothing. She could defend herself, though, because she also was a black belt in karate.

Harriet, knowing that her daughter had a bit of a rebellious nature, tried to always give her choices and talk to her about the best way to attract attention. She would ask, "Will you use your brains, beauty, or booty?" Harriet continued to suggest that Rachael tone down her manner of dress, but her daughter was stubborn and would have her own way. In the end, Harriet carefully chose her fights with the children, because, up to that point, they hadn't given her any serious problems.

Harriet was more concerned with helping Rachael overcome her glossophobia, the fear of public speaking. Rachael hated speaking in public, yet most of her school activities required some public speaking. Harriet hired a speech therapist to help her, which enabled her to give the required valedictory speech at graduation extremely well.

Rachael was the captain of Bentley's girls' varsity basketball team. Many colleges offered her full athletic scholarships.

Even before Rachael attended college, she'd begun making a difference. One day she'd come home from a long day at Bentley. Her mother was the only other person at home. Harriet was in the kitchen making one of her beautifully decorated cakes that everyone always raved about and some cherry-flavored lemonade, which was Rachael's favorite drink. Harriet was in a good mood and shared some of her good thoughts and lemonade with her daughter.

It seemed that Rachael was really irritated about something, so Harriet asked, "What's wrong?"

Rachael said, "We have a great girls' basketball team, but the boys' team has the better practice area, and it gets most of the funding and attention.

"That's discrimination."

Harriet's reply was, "Maybe it's time someone does something about that."

Harriet and Rachael learned that their concerns about possible gender discrimination were backed by the U.S. Constitution (Section 1983) and Title IX, a federal educational amendment signed into law in 1972. So mother and daughter wrote a letter to the school's principal, sending a copy to the school's superintendent.

Harriet was aware that if that type of injustice went unchecked, it could have a negative and long-term psychological effect on Rachael and all other girls who chose to play the sport. The school was quick to respond by first apologizing and then immediately correcting the situation.

Although Rachael and her mom liked Bentley overall, they'd felt a strong need to challenge this policy, even if it meant risking everything that Rachael had achieved there. Harriet was proud of her daughter and her sense of justice. She believed that one day, Rachael would be an excellent human- rights attorney. Rachael was always interested in the law and to the ways it could right wrongs.

After high school, Rachael entered Washington University; like her older brother, she majored in political science. Although she was crazy about boys, she was not seeing anyone special. She had broken up with her high school sweetheart, David Baum, three months earlier. She'd told her best friend, Janice, that he'd always tried to pressure her into having sex with him, and she just wasn't ready for that yet. She didn't want to be like many of her friends, who'd settled for someone and then stayed in unhappy relationships just to have a man. Rachael had decided to be patient and selective about whom she let into her heart and life.

"Choices are the hinges of destiny."

—Edwin Markham and Pythagoras

CHAPTER 10:
GEORGE'S FASCINATION

In 1986, George was a sixteen-year-old eleventh-grade honors student at Brooklyn's University High School. He often played at the community center where his father had been killed. Harriet pleaded with him to stay away from that area, but he ignored her. He became friends with some boys there and began hanging out with them.

George was attracted to this part of town, because it just seemed more exciting. There were so many things to do. Girls in George's classes at school thought he was very handsome. He could have easily had his pick, but for some reason he chose Latoya, even though she was not as smart or as pretty as most of the girls in school. At sixteen, he lost his virginity to her. In fact, only three months into the relationship, she thought she was pregnant. He later learned that it was a false alarm, but it was also a wake-up call for both of them. It reminded him of why his Christian faith was so important. His minister had always preached that premarital sex was wrong and sinful in the eyes of God.

Premarital sex was common. Many Christians accepted

that it was a sin to engage in sex before marriage, but some teenagers, including George, believed that if they used protection, it was okay. Rev. Davis, whose advice and counsel helped many youths straighten up, came to the house on several occasions. He believed he could help George see how premarital sex could adversely affect him and his family.

During his sexual encounters with Latoya, George used protection, and although he enjoyed having sex with her, he knew something was wrong. She was still hanging out and probably sleeping with Shank, her old boyfriend. George wondered if a person could be in love with two people at the same time. Latoya's response was, "No, but you can be torn between two lovers. It may be that one is for love and the other is to satisfy your lust. The one you want to be with the rest of your life is the one you love."

Rasheed's advice to George was that maybe she was confused: "It could be that she has feelings for one guy, but she is physically attracted to both of you."

George began to think that his religious faith might have some validity and that maybe his parents had known what they were doing when they'd chosen to follow their parents' faith. He decided he was going to listen to his mother more and try to follow her advice, especially about premarital sex.

As his mother liked to remind him, "You may be six feet tall, but you are still a child." Perhaps she was right about this after all.

Still George's behavior made Harriet feel as though she was losing control of her son, although she was very successful with her other two children and was very much in demand at parenting meetings at the Restoration. She finally gave in to the thought that maybe George would feel more comfortable discussing his problems with someone other than her, so she took him to talk with one of her best friends, Dr. Joyce Brown, a mental-health therapist.

Harriet she was failing George. The other two children had had a rough period of sadness and crying after their father's death, but they'd made the adjustment and moved forward. Harriet believed with all her heart that George would not have become so rebellious and made such bad choices if Leonard were alive. She felt totally responsible for George's behavior. She missed having Leonard there to talk to the children. She missed his companionship, love, support, and his sense of humor. She could have used his help with George, because he was turning away from his family and getting more involved with a gang. Family members and friends tried to help, but all their efforts fell on deaf ears. George seemed determined to ruin his life.

George's new family, the Blades, had given him a new name, Turk. Although "Turk" wanted to fit in, he was like a fish out of water in most cases, because he was educated and had different morals. This was especially true when the gang went out to commit crimes. George knew that he did not have to rob anyone to survive. He was from a middle-class household with plenty of food, clothing, shelter, support, and medical care, plus love from his family and friends. The gang members teased him for using proper English and for being a straight-A student at one of Brooklyn's best high schools. Because he was different, at times he felt that he had to prove that he was one of the boys, that he had what it took to be a Blade.

The gang needed money to buy beer, liquor, cigarettes, food, drugs, clothes, and especially new Adidas. They didn't care whom they robbed. It could be a senior citizen, a woman walking alone on a dimly lit street, or a well-dressed professional man. It could be a local or those men who came to visit prostitutes or a particular store or to just hail a taxi.

One Friday—payday for the working folks—the gang was running low on funds. They came up with a plan to rob a few people on their way home from work on the A train. The Blades had some strategies. First, wait until 6:00 when the train would be crowded, making it difficult for the transit police or an unsuspecting victim to catch them. Next, they figured if they robbed as a group of six, it would be highly unlikely for victims to make a positive ID, especially of all of them. They would snatch purses or briefcases as they ran through the front and back doors of the moving trains and then put the loot in a big paper shopping bag so no one would see them with the stolen items.

Another part of their plan was to get off the train at the next stop and immediately take the next train going in the opposite direction. Once they'd returned to their base, an abandoned building on the corner of Patchen Avenue and Bainbridge Street, they'd count the money and add it to the stash. They would keep driver's licenses and credit cards, using them once to charge merchandise before discarding them. Then it would be time to party. Someone would go out and get beer, liquor, cigarettes, drugs, and take-out.

George participated in the Friday robbing spree and thought it was fun. A week later, the gang decided to rob the D train, which also ran to and from Brooklyn and Manhattan, just in a different section of the city. As they were running and passing stolen merchandise to one another, a quick-thinking transit police officer caught up with George and arrested him. Everyone else, being much more experienced than George, got away; he was the only one in the gang without an arrest record and the only one caught that day.

George was taken into custody and booked for robbery

and assault. When he was told he was allowed one call, he
phoned his mother. She was devastated and heartbroken by
the news. Harriet quickly realized that she was now, indeed,
the only parent he had. She took a few deep breaths as the
tears welled up in her eyes, and then she composed herself.
She didn't want to ask her son why he seemed to have a desire
to self-destruct; she was more interested in finding out how
this had happened to her son, who had so much love to give
and such a bright future ahead of him. After offering George
some words of comfort, she hung up the phone and began
questioning whether she had the necessary parenting skills to
help her son get back on track. She wasn't sure what his needs
were anymore.

Harriet called some political friends, as well as the family's
minister, and they all rushed to the police precinct. George
was released to his mother's custody with the promise that he
would return to the Brooklyn criminal court on the following
Monday. Harriet did not want to lose her son to the streets,
so she put him on lockdown. He was restricted to the house
for the rest of that weekend. She showed him some tough
love, making it clear that if he left the house that weekend, she
would call the police to take him back to jail.

Fortunately, George still had respect for his living
grandparents. After talking to them, he reluctantly followed
their advice and stayed away from that neighborhood the
whole weekend. When he went to court the following Monday
morning, the judge told George that he knew of his father
and believed him to have been a great man. He asked, "Why
do you want to bring shame on your fine family, George?"
George didn't answer. The judge noted that this was George's
first offense, so he gave him two years of probation, on
the condition that George continued to see a mental-health

therapist. The judge then released George to his mother's supervision.

George had dodged a bullet.

But three months passed, and Harriet received another late-night call from George. He was at the police precinct again. She rushed down to get her son, except this time things were different. While he and the gang were in the process of robbing passengers on a train, an elderly lady was hurt and had to go to the hospital. Because George was still in the early stages of his probation, Harriet could not just take him home.

Just before his sentencing, George told the judge, "Your Honor, I learned my lesson from this." The judge quickly replied, "No, you didn't, because if you did, you would not be here now. You had already been given a chance, but you, like many young men your age, will only learn after you have been incarcerated."

George was sentenced to six months on Staten Island. He had hoped that if he did go to jail, the judge would send him to one closer to home, but the judge said he had to take into consideration the available space. He read the terms and conditions of the sentence and sent George on his way. George's mother and siblings stood in the courtroom, clearly heartbroken, but they still managed to wave good-bye. Feeling helpless, with tears rolling down their cheeks, they went home without George.

George was sent back to the temporary holding cell with other prisoners. There, the bus came to pick them up to take them to prison. It looked like a regular school bus, except it was gray and had a chicken-wire cage of thick metal separating the passengers and the driver. The prisoners made their way from Brooklyn to Staten Island.

Once there, the prisoners had to submit to a second round

of fingerprinting and mug shots, plus a thorough strip search. Their personal belongings were taken, tagged, and put into storage. The next step was taking a shower and getting prison attire. The facility didn't always have the right size, but George was lucky that clothing in his size was available. Sometimes the clothes issued were too tight, which attracted the attention of other inmates who interpreted tight clothing as a sign of homosexuality. Inmates were not allowed to have belts in their pants or strings in their shoes, a precaution against suicide by hanging.

Copying prison culture wearing stringless sneakers—called "felon sneakers" by those in law enforcement—became a common style for youth outside prison walls. In the early '90s, beltless pants also became a style among young people, called "sagging pants." Parents who knew that "felon sneakers" and "sagging pants" were part of the prison culture rebelled against their children's adaptation of this style.

One of the correctional officers, known as COs, walked George to his new home and locked him in his cell. George introduced himself to his cellmate: "Hey man, I'm Turk."

"Th-th-they ca-ca-call me-B-B-Beast," the inmate stuttered in reply. He was sitting on the edge of his bunk, reading a book. The huge black man looked almost super human: his well chiseled muscles appeared as if he'd lifted weights all his life.

George stood silently, looking at Beast for a moment, and then asked, "Which bed is mine?" Beast pointed to the top bunk. Turk saw there were no covers or pillow on the top bed, but the bed where Beast was sitting had two of everything— pillows, sheets, and blankets. George asked Beast if he could have his bedding, and Beast told him that if he wanted that stuff, he would have to "be his girl." George looked at him as if he were crazy and said, "What the fuck you mean, man?"

"Jus-jus-just like I said—if you want this stu-stuff, you will have to be my bi-bitch," replied Beast.

George said, "Fuck it, then, you can keep that shit."

"You are gon-gonna be my bi-bitch anyway," Beast said. "You can make the shit hard if you wanna."

George ignored that last statement and attempted to climb the ladder to the top bed. Beast grabbed him and punched him in the mouth. George, a third-degree black belt in karate, hit him back, but Beast was too big, too strong, and he hit too hard. Though athletic and young, George's slender frame was outmatched. He yelled for the guard.

"Shut the fuck up," Beast demanded. "The guards aren't coming down here unless I call them. Now, I want you to take those clothes off and put on these panties." He tossed a pair of pink woman's panties on George's bed.

George stood there with his nose and mouth bleeding, his eyes beginning to swell, and his head aching badly. Beast told him, "If you don't put on these panties, I'll have no choice but to do you like I did my last cellmate." He hesitated for a moment and added, "I broke his jaw, and they put him in the hospital." Beast then said, "Hell, it ain't gonna be that bad— they gonna cut me loose in three days. Just put on the panties, and I won't bother you till tomorrow night." George refused, and they scuffled again, but this time George put some hurt on Beast.

Beast told George he had until the next day.

"I have a headache and need to see a doctor," George told his imposing cellmate. Beast called the doctor.

The doctor, Herman "Hey Doc" Wolonaski, was in prison as a result of a malpractice that resulted in the death of a young woman while he was giving her an abortion. That was not the first time his practices had been in question or caused others to suffer. It finally caught up with him and he wound up in prison. The warden decided that his expertise could be utilized in the prison, the same as the chef who was serving time and preparing meals for prisoners.

While they waited for the doctor, Beast told George, "That doctor is an inmate, and he was once my cellmate. Sometimes he gives you the wrong medicine on purpose so he can knock you out."

Within a few minutes, the doctor came in, looked at the wounds, gave George a pill, and also secretly slipped him a shiv, a homemade knife. George took the pill, despite Beast's warning, and his headache started to ease immediately. Without his pillow and covers, George went up to bed. But he could not sleep. He was busy thinking of ways he could defend himself if Beast tried to attack him again. He felt confident he could successfully defend himself now that he had a weapon.

George had learned in one of his science classes which arteries bleed the fastest if punctured. About an hour passed, and Beast figured George was knocked out from the medicine. Beast eased his way up to George's bed and started pulling at his pants. While Beast was doing that, George lay still, pretending to be asleep. He was well aware of what Beast was trying to do. As soon as Beast pulled down George's pants enough where he thought he could rape him, George rose up and stuck the shiv into Beast's neck. Although it was dark, there was just enough light for George to stick Beast in the right place.

The sharp blade sliced open Beast's left carotid artery; blood gushed out like water from a faucet on full blast. Beast fell off the top bunk onto the cell floor, screaming at the top of his lungs. His voice soon became just low moans as he lay there, helpless in a pool of his own blood. COs came and called the prison medics, who took Beast to the prison hospital, he died en route. One of the COs whispered to George, "Don't worry, Beast had this coming to him. It's obvious this is a case of self-defense."

The COs mopped up Beast's blood and left George in the cell overnight. After being questioned by prison authorities, George finally went to bed and slept without worrying about being attacked. Beast was no longer a threat to his manhood, but, still, George was saddened that he had killed a man. However, he remembered what his karate mentor, his sensei, had always told him: "If you kill someone while protecting your own life in a fight that you did not start, it is justified in the eyes of the law, as well as in the eyes of God. So you must forgive yourself and move on."

George breathed a great sigh of relief, because he didn't have to submit to Beast. He'd known that Beast would die from the wound he'd inflicted. The prison authorities did a quick investigation and determined that this was a clear case of self-defense. Being in a cell with no partner suited George fine. He certainly did not want to go through that ordeal again.

Soon after Beast was taken to the prison morgue, everyone went back to sleep. They all knew they had to get up early and prepare for breakfast lineup. Turk was used to going to bed early at home. He and his siblings rarely stayed up after 11:00 during the week, so going to bed early was not a big adjustment for him.

The next morning, as the prisoners were heading to the prison cafeteria, some of them noticed George's swollen face. Most of them were surprised to learn that it was Beast who had gone to the morgue. Prisoners treated George like he was a hero. As he walked in line, they yelled things like, "You're the man, Turk!" and "You're the boss man now!" He was not a full-grown man, yet he'd challenged and successfully defeated the prison's toughest and most brutal inmate.

George was glad to get into the cafeteria, because he'd missed dinner the night before. He noticed that the place was clean, and the food looked like the food he ate at home. For breakfast that morning, inmates were treated to scrambled eggs, pork sausages, cinnamon buns, and orange juice. Turk was sitting on the end of a long table with the seats attached, getting ready to eat, when he noticed someone staring at him. It was a thin, light-skinned guy with a beard who was wearing a black-and-white knit brimless, rounded cap called a kufi. George had seen this type of cap worn by some Muslims in the 'hood. He wondered why this man was staring at him; George was not Muslim.

The man got up from his table, came over to George, and introduced himself as Malik Muhammad. He asked George, "Are those pork sausages on your plate?"

Turk looked down at the sausages and, in his best slang, said, "Yeah."

Malik said, "Man, you shouldn't eat pork 'cause it ain't good for you."

Then Malik reached down, grabbed the sausages from George's plate and started walking away. While George was still watching him, Malik took about three or four steps from the table and started eating the sausages.

George stood up and asked Malik, "Hey, man, what the fuck are you doing?" The COs rushed over to the table, got between the two inmates, and told George that if he didn't sit down and shut up, they were going to remove him. George was hungry but did not want any more trouble, so he sat down and asked one of the COs to bring him some more sausages.

The CO said, "I'll see what I can do." A few minutes later,

the CO came back with four sausages wrapped in a napkin and put them on George's plate.

George said, "Thanks, man."

The CO replied, "You better keep your ass outta trouble, man, or you will be in here forever."

Just about everyone in that prison was happy that Beast had not survived the fight with George, because he was no longer a threat to anyone. His family could not afford a funeral with a burial, so they had him cremated. He was not a church member, so the services were held in a funeral parlor with its director, Livingston Demise, giving the eulogy.

"It seemed Qualeb was doomed from the start," said Demise. "In addition to being black and poor, he had a speech impediment. He stuttered, and that was never addressed. Instead of helping him, we teased and made fun of him; even his teachers wrote him off as a tragic burden to society. This made it very difficult for him to function as a productive member of society. So, in his mind, he used the only attributes he had to survive. He used his physical strength and power to rape, to rob, and to kill others. Prison was his home, and when he came out, it was as though he were only on vacation until he committed some crime that would put him back in prison. He was the opposite of most of us so-called normal people in that prison had become his home, and the outside world was a place to vacation. Many of you seem surprised to hear this, but many others in here know that this is the condition of many young black men and women throughout this country."

George remembered that something weird had happened during the investigation of the fight. He'd overheard the prison officials refer to Beast as Mr. Qualeb Poppytail. The name had sounded familiar, but George couldn't place it. Then, it occurred to him—this was the same man who'd shot and killed his father! The district attorney's office was convinced that this was just a coincidence, because when he'd first heard Qualeb's real name, George hadn't known who the attorney was talking about.

George was confused. At first he had felt sad that he had taken a man's life, even though it was in self-defense. Those feelings turned to joy and relief that he had avenged his father's death.

George had also learned that his father's murder case was in jeopardy because one of the two witnesses, Skip, had disappeared three months after Leonard's death, and the other witness, Butch, was withdrawing his story, because he was afraid to testify. That was how Beast had ended up in the same prison with Turk and the reason he'd said, "They gonna cut me loose in three days."

The Brooklyn district attorney's office could no longer legally hold Beast on the charge. It was a good thing—and some might say a miraculous or just thing—that Turk had helped him meet his fate. Otherwise, Beast may have gotten away with murder and been released to commit more crimes.

"God, grant me the serenity to accept the things I cannot change, the courage to change the things I can, and the wisdom to know the difference."

—Reinhold Niebuhr

CHAPTER 11:
GEORGE'S FREEDOM
MAY NOT BE SO EASY

Harriet was doing everything in her power to free George from prison. Some powerful politicians, several civil rights organizations that dealt with human-rights issues, and a few powerful attorneys from the community offered assistance. After an initial meeting, the parties filed a writ of habeas corpus, a summons forcing a court order demanding that a prisoner be taken before the court to challenge the original evidence. If flaws were found in the evidence, a prisoner could be released immediately and cleared of all charges. The hearing was set for a week from the date it was filed.

Harriet, Rasheed, and Rachael were hoping, praying, and doing all they could to get George home. It had only been a little more than a year since they'd lost their great husband and father, Leonard Jr. They wanted to do everything in their power to avoid losing their son and brother, George.

For George, the week seemed to be the longest of his short life. He couldn't talk to anyone in the prison about what was being done on his behalf, because if other prisoners thought he was receiving special treatment, they might try to prevent his release by provoking him into a fight. So he had to be very careful and stay out of trouble.

The week was uneventful, however; George quickly learned that in prison, playing basketball was almost a surefire way to get in trouble. Each game erupted in fighting, verbal and physical. On the outside, George was used to arguments and an occasional fistfight during a game, but nothing like this. This was not just a basketball game; it was a test of manhood and heart. If a prisoner showed any sign of weakness, another would come after him like a shark smelling blood.

During one game, George dribbled the ball and made a two-point layup. As he was coming down, Malik crashed into him. George held his ankle and hopped off the court. He didn't have a major injury, but this gave him the much-needed excuse to get out of the game. Although George loved basketball, he knew this activity could cause the type of trouble that would put his freedom in jeopardy, so he left the game behind.

While waiting for the hearing, it seemed that every day brought an opportunity for George to sabotage his chances for early release. The day after the incident with Beast, he went to use the only public telephone available to prisoners to call his family. Prisoners were only allowed three minutes each on the telephone, and a young black prisoner named Charles Butler was in the middle of his brief call. One other person stood in line ahead of George, a Hispanic man, about five-feet, five-inches tall and about one hundred thirty pounds. He kept telling Charles to hurry up, because his time had been up five minutes earlier, but Charles continued talking. The little Hispanic man left, but he returned a few minutes later with about six other Hispanic men who all came running past George. The next thing George knew, Charles was grabbing his chest and yelling for help, bleeding profusely from a wound.

By the time the COs reached the scene, Charles had dropped helplessly to his knees, and the Hispanic men were nowhere to be seen. The COs asked George to tell them what had happened. He told them what he'd seen, but he could not identify any of the attackers, because the attack had happened so fast. The COs escorted George back to his cell and then closed phone privileges for the rest of the day. George would not have put his own life in jeopardy by snitching on those guys, even if he could have identified them. He felt it was the prison's responsibility to have supervision in that area.

Although it had been just another day in the life of seasoned prisoners, George was unable to sleep that night. He could not help thinking about the horrible things that could happen to him in prison. He wondered why he'd put himself in this situation in the first place. Then he reflected on the events of his sixteen years.

He thought about whether he wanted to follow in his father's footsteps and become a leader in the community, continuing to follow the Christian faith, or to create his own path and become a famous rapper.

He was confused about how his life was turning out. He'd learned that Beast was the man who'd shot and killed his father. He had avenged his father's death without even knowing it. That alone was a lot to wrap his brain around, but he couldn't help thinking about the things he loved about life in Bedford-Stuyvesant. The rap movement was just beginning, and he loved the whole music scene.

His parents had sent him to music school to learn structured and traditional music. Hip-hop was improvisation, making up rhymes and music as the song is created. He was good at this skill and was beginning to make a name for himself within the music community. Nonetheless, he came to the conclusion that the price he had to pay for that lifestyle was too much—and the outcome could cost him his life.

The next day, George finally had a chance to call his mother. He told her about the fight with Beast, and she told him, "The prison authorities told us yesterday, but they would not allow us a visit because two deaths occurred in two days. We love you. Please be very careful. We are doing all we can to get you out of there." George assured her that he had definitely learned his lesson and that when he got out, he would never do anything that would put him back in prison. She was ecstatic to hear that her son had come to his senses.

She told him, "We love you. Hang in there, and please stay out of trouble."

If things went right at the hearing, George would have only four more days of incarceration, but he couldn't help feeling as though he were walking in a minefield, where any little thing could blow apart.

It was now Thursday, and George was due in court that next Monday. Fortunately for him, some dramatic events were happening in the prison that he was not even aware of but that would affect his hearing.

George had not yet been given a job assignment, so that day the CO gave him a choice of going to the library, playing board games with other prisoners, or just staying in his cell. He chose to stay in his cell and reflect on his life a little more. It was really the first time he'd given serious thought to the goals he wanted for himself and the goals his family had set for him. For the most part, up until that point in his life, his parents had given him everything: his name, his religion, his morals, and, as is typical in most families, his personality and his belief system.

If God existed, Turk definitely needed him now. He began questioning why he believed in God and why he was a member of the Christian faith. He had been raised in the Christian tradition since he was a baby, but he hadn't decided within himself what he truly believed. He was now thinking, "What if I choose a different religion from my family? Would they still accept me and respect my decision?" He wanted to know more about his own religion as well as others, so he got permission to go to the prison's library and read about religions.

He read about the Tainos people of the Caribbean, who worshiped the spirits of their ancestors. He also read about an indigenous African people called the Yorubas. Many Yoruba people were brought to the Americas during the slave trade, along with other ethnic nationalities from Africa. The spiritually tolerant religious beliefs of the Yoruba were among the most recognizable African-derived traditions in the Americas, George learned. The Yorubas believed that when they died, they entered the realm of the ancestors, where they still had influence on Earth. [10]

Although many of these indigenous religions existed, four major religions were observed around the world, George discovered—Christianity (particularly Catholicism), Islam, Judaism, and Hinduism. He read about each of them and decided that the Christian faith was the best choice for him, because he identified with the doctrine of forgiveness, making amends, and repentance, which is practiced in its members' everyday lives.

"Every choice carries a consequence. For better or worse, each choice is the unavoidable consequence of its predecessor. There are not exceptions. If you can accept that a bad choice carries the seed of its own punishment, why not accept the fact that a good choice yields desirable fruit?"

—Gary Ryan Blair

CHAPTER 12:
MORE TROUBLE IN PARADISE

If prisoners in a particular cell block received a score for good behavior of seventy-five or above, they were treated to a movie on Saturday night. George was housed in the gang unit. This unit had earned seventy-six points, so those inmates got a chance to see *Lock Up*, a 1989 prison film starring Sylvester Stallone and Donald Sutherland, on a fifty-two-inch projection screen. The room only held one hundred prisoners, who would be seated in rows of folding chairs ten seats across and ten seats deep. The inmates were warned that any talking during the movie would cause them all to return to their cells without seeing the rest of the movie.

The film started at 7:00 sharp. The lights went off, and everyone fell silent. Everything went great for the first hour and five minutes of the movie. Then someone threw a brick up into the air, which landed on a prisoner's head just two rows in front of George. The lights came on, and the movie stopped. Though prisoners normally didn't snitch on each other, several offered to point out the guy who threw the brick if they could see the rest of the film. The COs agreed and took Alfred Sistrunk to the prison "hole." He would be out of the population with no privileges and very few visitors for a long time.

George prayed to get to court Monday morning and for things to go in his favor. He was down to just one more day in hell. On Sunday morning, right after breakfast, the inmates went to the prison church. Malik was sitting up front, about four rows ahead of George, and he became disruptive, because it was a Christian church service. He accused the white prison chaplain of trying to indoctrinate black prisoners into European religious beliefs and values, which resulted in his being put in the hole for two days.

"God enters by a private door into each individual."

—*Ralph Waldo Emerson*

CHAPTER 13:
GEORGE HAS HIS DAY IN COURT

On Monday morning, everything was delayed. The bus that carried prisoners back and forth from prison to court was a half-hour late. Once they were on the highway, they sat in traffic jams, causing them to reach court an hour later than usual. Luckily for George, the judge sitting on the bench that day was none other than Judge Joe Bright. Judge Bright had a reputation for impartially considering the cases against all blacks, whites, and Hispanics who came to his court. He reviewed the evidence and took into consideration the person's previous record. Some said he should have recused himself in this case because he knew George's family.

Judge Bright took George into his chambers to talk. He could see that George was an extremely intelligent young man who could be a great asset to his community someday. The judge advised George to lose the nickname and anything else that associated him with the Blades gang. Then Judge Bright made George promise he would never go back to his old gang buddies.

George was released and went back to being just plain George rather than "Turk." A month passed without any problems. George went back to school and continued to excel, making good grades and staying away from the gang neighborhood as he'd promised. It was almost time for schools to close for the Christmas holidays when Harriet got a call from one of Judge Bright's friends, Dr. Adam Cadd. Dr. Cadd was a seasoned architect and a retired professor in the school of architecture at Howard University in Washington, D.C. He was now a very successful director of that program. He was also once an active member of the Wilsons' own First Baptist Church.

Dr. Cadd asked Harriet if she'd let George spend most of the holiday break with him and his family. He wanted to see if he could interest George in the field of architecture design.

Although no classes were in session at Howard University during the holidays, the campus was still open to all personnel and students. Dr. Cadd gave George a tour of the school and introduced him to students who came in during the holidays to complete projects. He asked one of the senior students, William Barnes, to mentor George for a couple of days. George saw that his life would be much more productive as an architect than a rapper, so he made the decision to put his energy into becoming an architect. Although his mother could afford to pay for his education, he hoped that his past bad choices wouldn't prevent him from getting a full scholarship to attend Howard University. After spending nearly two weeks with Dr. Cadd, George became convinced that he could make a contribution to the world. He assured his family he was definitely back on track in life.

George wondered why his old girlfriend Latoya never contacted him or returned his calls. Whenever he called her house, she was never home. He wanted to talk to her, because while he was incarcerated he'd begun wondering about the type of relationship they really had. George also remembered that she'd been acting strange just before he was arrested. A couple of times she'd asked to meet him at a particular place, but then didn't show up. And he'd caught her in a lie when she'd told him she was going to California to spend a weekend with her father. He'd known she was lying, because he'd seen her each of those days. Plus, she'd told him once before that her dad lived in Harlem, not California.

George missed Latoya, so he decided to call her again. This time, she answered.

"Hey, Latoya, what's going on? I've been trying to reach you."

She said, "I've gone back with Shank."

George had always felt a little suspicious of the relationship between Latoya and Shank, because she spent as much time with him as with George. He knew that it would be pointless to ask why she hadn't told him early in their relationship that she was still seeing Shank. It could have been that she'd wanted to have two guys fight over her, he thought.

A little later that day,

Latoya called George and asked him to meet her at their favorite place, the McDonald's on Stuyvesant and Decatur avenues.

They met, ate burgers, and chatted for a while. Then she confided in him about her troubled past. First, she told him that she had sickle cell anemia, a hereditary disease in which red blood cells form an abnormal crescent shape, producing great pain.

It can be very painful, often lead to various infections and other severe complications, even resulting in death.

She explained that her illness had flared up and she became ill. This kept her from wanting to see or talk to anyone. She told George, "Sometimes it makes me very tired and other times it is so painful that I've seriously considered suicide. I feel much better now that I've gotten help from a support group called Sickle Cell Anemia Consultants. They're great at teaching me how to manage it and at making me feel better about myself."

Latoya went on to tell George that she really had only seen her father once in her life, and she often wondered if he'd ever wanted her in the first place. She also questioned whether her mother had tricked her dad into impregnating her. Her mother had always talked badly about her father.

"I only know her side," Latoya admitted. "I wish I could get to know who he is before he dies. I believe I have sex to feel like I am getting love from my dad. Does that make sense?"

George said, "I guess it does. But the question is how you are going to resolve this?"

"I don't know," she replied. "The only male I'm close to is my brother, and he's gay."

George said, "Latoya, I'll always be there if you ever need someone to talk to. Don't get me wrong, I'm not judging you or your family. I was just raised differently, and I want to keep my family's values and traditions."

They gave each other a big hug and went their separate ways.

George knew that he had to concentrate on his next move. He had learned a lot of hard lessons during the past year. Although he loved hip-hop music, Dr. Cadd had introduced him to architecture design, and that was the focus of his passion. He knew a gang like the Blades would turn on anyone who was not 100 percent committed to them and to their culture. He couldn't allow that attitude to affect his decisions about the future, because he did not agree with most of what they did. He especially disagreed with the criminal aspect of their activity. He also learned that being a prisoner locked up in jail is like being a slave forced to work on a plantation: their freedom is gone, and prisoners suffer immediate consequences when they don't do as they're told. No sane person would want to be incarcerated. George knew that if he studied and applied himself, he could achieve his educational goals.

George made an introspective decision. The experience of going to prison hadn't left George unchanged, but the change was positive. He realized what effect his negative behavior had had on his family, his career goals, and his community, not to mention the threat to his life and independence. He also realized how blessed he was to have loving parents and siblings, real friends in his own neighborhood, and a community that felt as though it had a vested interest in his success. Another important lesson he'd learned was that healing can follow misfortunes and mistakes. Even if someone came apart, that person could reunite with his or her family as a stronger person because of the lessons learned from experience.

No one in the community criticized George or beat him down for making a mistake. They did, however, remind him that his parents had made great contributions to Bed-Stuy. His community recognized that he had the ability to have the same impact, but only if he desired it. It did seem ironic that his father, who'd, believed so strongly in revitalization—a new life for a poor area like the Wilsons' Harlem neighborhood—was murdered while attempting to find ways to help erase the poverty there. Leonard had gone to that community youth center knowing the visit carried risks, but he'd been willing to face those dangers to serve the people. He, along with a majority of those living in that area, had wanted to change the neighborhood culture. They'd wanted to create a standard where people could live with respect, without fear of being accosted or threatened. George's father had wanted to help make it a place where people could live productive and useful lives. He'd believed that if people could support those willing to grow, to contribute, and to change, the neighborhood itself would also mature, that people needed hope and a helping hand to look beyond their own problems.

"Getting over a painful experience is much like crossing monkey bars. You have to let go at some point in order to move forward."

—*Unknown*

CHAPTER 14:
TEN YEARS AFTER DR. WILSON'S DEATH

Ten years after Leonard's untimely death, the Wilson family has finally experienced relative peace in their lives again. Harriet, age sixty and still very attractive, remains single. She and Dr. Benjamin Hartsfield, a widower, neighbor, and high school principal, have become close friends, but Harriet has never believed that her relationship with Leonard can be duplicated.

The children have moved on with their lives, as well. Thirty-year-old Rasheed is a corporate attorney and married to Ebony, a criminal defense attorney who was his childhood sweetheart. They have a two-year-old son named Omar. Rasheed and Ebony bought a four-story gray stone house on McDonough Street in Stuyvesant Heights so they could remain close to their childhood friends. Rachael, twenty-eight, is a civil rights attorney. She married an assistant district attorney, Charles Adams, and is expecting their first child. They also opted to purchase a house on the same block as her brother.

George, twenty-six, is engaged to his college sweetheart, Gabriele Kaiser. He is an assistant architect with the New York

State Department of Environmental Conservation as well as a mentor to boys and girls at the Bed-Stuy Youth Center. Working with the neighborhood children has given him a better insight into the challenges parents face today. During George's youth, felon sneakers and sagging pants made parents crazy; today, it is just the sagging pants.

George doesn't pull any punches when he talks about his experience and his former lifestyle. He tells the kids at the center about their choices: they can go to traditional, accredited universities or trade schools and prepare themselves to work in chosen careers, or they can write business plans and become entrepreneurs.

The alternative, according to George, is to attend Dumb Ass University, or DAU. Students who attend this school are delinquents, criminals, and those who don't have a desire to improve themselves. They will eventually graduate into prison, the grave, a mental institution, or one underpaying job after another. Entrance requirements for DAU are very low:

1. First, people must give up who they are, their dreams, and their education by becoming a member of a gang, like the Blades. They must blindly follow any and all commands of their new leaders.

2. People should reject traditional schools and their brand of education to allow the streets to serve as classrooms and gang leaders as teachers. People's assignments are to commit crimes without getting caught.

3. People cannot wear belts or have strings in their shoes or sneakers. This way, should they get arrested, other prison inmates will know they are down with them.

4. People must give up their biological families to embrace their new gang families. Gang leaders will give them a new moral compass and become their new parents.

Other gang members will become their siblings, duty-bound to protect each other.

George decided he would help as many youth as possible channel some of the energy they put toward sports and entertainment toward formal education or business training. He knew firsthand that too many youth are on the wrong path, which is leading them right into the hands of the criminal justice system.

In cities with large African-American and Hispanic populations, there always seems to be emphasis on building new prisons, but not nearly enough focus on helping failing youths and communities, or retraining those adults who have lost their jobs to overseas workers. Society seems to have its priorities backward; being reactive instead of proactive. People need to better understand the culture and mentality of those in the 'hood so they may find ways to create an atmosphere of hope and support, coupled with a dose of reality and communication from the wise.

"Change your thoughts and you change your world."
—*Norman Vincent Peale*

CHAPTER 15:
CONCLUSION

Even with strong love and support, George lost his way after his father was senselessly killed in an armed robbery, becoming intrigued with street life.

George forgot all the values and traditions his parents and community had instilled in him. He made the decision to seek acceptance from his boys in the streets rather than his family, community, and himself. He went astray and crossed the line, predictably landing in jail. There, his life was always in imminent danger. Although his prison stint was short, he was able to examine his life and to decide which route he would ultimately take.

George came to realize that he was blessed to have a family that loved him very much, even when he made big mistakes. He knew that when he was a little boy, although his misbehavior was sometimes annoying to his family, they never stopped loving him. He also knew that if he was ever tempted to return to the streets, he had many people who could help him get back on the right track. George found hope and a helping hand by talking to someone he trusted—his mother—and asking

God for help when facing temptations.

From this experience, he learned that he did not have to prove his manliness by getting involved in criminal activity, being heartless, taking advantage of the weak, or just being plain selfish and self-centered. Life was not about what someone wears on the outside, but what's on the inside. Building character—by growing integrity, work ethic, decency, kindness, generosity—is what everyone must do on his or her life's journey. People aren't able to take the cars, jewelry, clothes, or gold teeth with them when they depart this life—only take the essence of their characters, their souls.

George learned that he had a conscience, that inner voice that would help him judge the morality of his actions. It would guide him to know and to follow God's law by doing well and avoiding evil. When he had to make a decision, his conscience would serve as a guide to the best decisions.

"It takes courage to grow up and become who you really are."

—E. E. Cummings

AFTERWORD

In one of his community meetings, Reverend Mitchell told the group people gathered that people are poor for different reasons. Often they find themselves in a situation beyond their control. Sometimes people are poor because of their behavior or their culture. In fairness, white people aren't responsible for all the shortcomings and problems of black people. We all have to take responsibility for themselves decisions and choices that we make—whatever race, color, religion, or nationality we are. I have learned that not all white people are my enemies and not all black people are my friends. There are many cases where black people have failed to take responsibility for themselves and have done things that kept themselves poor. Some examples are (1) dropping out of school and not having the right goals, (2) making the decision to rob others because they weren't taught better, or they don't want to work for a living, (3) selling drugs because it's easy, fast money (thereby not only bringing crime to their neighborhood but making addicts out of their customers), (4) choosing to milk/defraud the social services system because it's widely accepted and easy, and (5) not instilling the right values or morals in their children.

What would happen if our youth took the energy they use for sports and entertainment and put it into education or training to become architects engineers or business owners? Not everyone is cut out to be a doctor or lawyer, but there are obviously many other areas where people can become successful and productive. Any job that provides a decent, honest income is one to aspire to. Too many of our youth are on the wrong path, and it is leading them right into the hands of the criminal justice system, which will gladly make a place for them.

We need to better understand the culture and mentality of those in the 'hood so we may find ways to create an atmosphere of hope and support, coupled with a dose of reality and communication from the wise.

Those who fought to change that culture knew that too many of our young men and women were looking for an easy way out, or a quick fix to their inherited poverty. Some youths put all their energy into playing basketball or football, hoping to get into a professional sports team. Today, the reality is that the probability of being drafted by the NBA is 3 in 10,000 for high school boys, and the odds for high school girls are 1 in 500. For the NFL, the probability is 8 in 10,000. In most cases, a student's grade point average is a key factor, which poses a problem for students from poor neighborhoods. On rare occasions, a talented athlete can beat those odds, but it doesn't happen very often.

A common fantasy among youth is becoming a musician, but according to rap artist Joseph "Fat Joe" Cartagena, the odds are 1 in 10 million. There are thousands and thousands of artists who want to be signed, but only a small percentage of new acts are successful. [11]

Some young people think they'll make their fortune in drugs, prostitution, or other types of crime. Most drug dealers and users end up dead or serving many years in jail. Prostitutes often succumb to sexually transmitted diseases or steady abuse. And, as George found out, muggers and robbers also end up in prison.

The question now becomes, "When do we change course and at least try a different strategy?"

It is also common knowledge that racism, committed consciously or unconsciously, still exists in our schools and places of employment, but we have to prepare ourselves and deal with racism as it comes.

The major disparities between blacks and whites are in education and economics. Instead of making every effort to close that gap, whites frequently blame blacks for not being able to achieve parity with whites in these areas. According to the National Urban League's annual State of Black America report, issued in July, 2010, "the last time the unemployment rate for whites was higher than 9% was in March 1983. At that time, black unemployment was 20.1%." We cannot fix poverty in America until we fix education. That "is the true path out of poverty," the report said. "Education is the civil-rights issue of our time." The report also concluded that the dropout rate from high school is 26% for Hispanic students and 13% for black students, versus 10.8 % for white students.

If black people quit fighting now, we could wind up back in slavery. In my opinion, serving time in jail is modern-day slavery. There is someone controlling your every move 24/7, 365 days a year.

The need to address this problem is urgent and this book is speaking to all fair-minded people to come together and help address and correct the situation. How do we do this? Contact all politicians in your community and see to it that these issues become priority. Your voice and your vote is your power, so use them.

We deserve better than this.

BIBLIOGRAPHY

1. http://urbanology.org/BedStuy/
2. The People of Brooklyn; A History of Two Neighborhoods, Brooklyn Educational Cultural Alliance, New York 1980 p.27
3. Ibid: p.3
4. "Andrew W. Cooper". Answers.com. Retrieved January 30, 2009.
5. Barry Stein, Rebuilding Bedford-Stuyvesant, Community Economic Development in the Ghetto, Center for Community Development, Cambridge, Massachusetts, 1975 p. 11
6. Lueck, Thomas J. (January 30, 2002). "Andrew W. Cooper, 74, Pioneering Journalist".
7. Ibid: p.2
8. Ibid: p.1
9. urbanology.org/BedStuy/
10. wikipedia.org/wiki/Taíno people, 7 March 2011
11. urblife.com/the-life/parent-trap-fat-joe

www.ingramcontent.com/pod-product-compliance
Lightning Source LLC
Chambersburg PA
CBHW071342130626
46556CB00005B/1987